Contents

Ladybird books are widely available, but in case of
difficulty may be ordered by post or telephone from:

Ladybird Books – Cash Sales Department
Littlegate Road Paignton Devon TQ3 3BE
Telephone 01803 554761

A catalogue record for this book is available
from the British Library

Published by Ladybird Books Ltd Loughborough Leicestershire UK
Ladybird Books Inc Auburn Maine 04210 USA

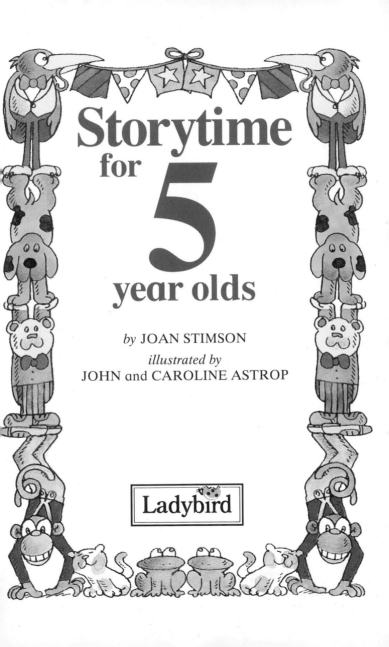

Storytime
for
5
year olds

by JOAN STIMSON

illustrated by
JOHN and CAROLINE ASTROP

Ladybird

Walter's red star

Walter the chimpanzee was excited. Today he was going to school with Andrew.

Each Friday Miss Nash allowed one child to bring in a pet. At last it was Andrew's turn. He was as excited as Walter.

Andrew sang all the way to school. Walter turned cartwheels on the pavement.

'Good heavens!' said Miss Nash. She had been expecting a rabbit or a tortoise.

Miss Nash had to think quickly.

'If Walter's too big for Pet's Corner,' she said, 'he can have Steven Smith's desk. Steven is absent with measles.'

Walter settled into Steven's place and Miss Nash called the register. Walter started to bang the lid of his desk. The children giggled.

'*Stop it, Walter!*' said Miss Nash. 'It's time to look at some numbers.'

The children groaned. Walter lifted the lid of his desk again. He found a bag of half-finished crisps. Walter ate them quietly. Then he blew up the bag and burst it.

Miss Nash almost jumped out of her seat. The children roared with laughter.

'Walter!' said Miss Nash. 'I won't tell you again. Now settle down, everybody.'

The children worked hard at their numbers. It was all double-dutch to Walter. But Jane Fletcher got ten out of ten. Miss Nash gave her a green star.

After break Miss Nash opened up the art cupboard. Out came paper, paints, crayons and Plasticine.

'This looks more interesting,' thought Walter.

'I want you to think of a spaceship,' said Miss Nash. 'Make a picture of it flying through the stars and past the planets.'

The children closed their eyes and thought. Then they started work.

Walter closed *his* eyes. Then he rummaged in his packed lunch. He stuck a banana to some paper with Plasticine.

'UGH!' cried the children.

'Good try, Walter,' said Miss Nash. At least Walter was quiet now.

Miss Nash gave a green star to Michael Ford. Michael had painted a big spaceship flying past a red planet, in a blue sky full of stars.

After lunch it was time for gym. Gym was Walter's best subject.

The class hopped and bounced to music. Miss Nash played the piano.

'Just copy Walter,' she said.

Suddenly there was a loud wail. The children gasped and pointed.

Heather Bennett had climbed the bars at the side of the gym. She wanted to touch the hall ceiling. Now she was frightened. Heather screamed and screamed.

'Keep calm, everybody,' said Miss Nash. But she didn't feel calm herself. Miss Nash didn't like heights.

Quick as a flash, Walter swung up the bars. He put his arm round Heather's waist and helped her down.

9

The children clapped and cheered. Heather sobbed.

'Well done, Walter!' said Miss Nash. She beamed with relief.

Miss Nash went to her classroom. She came back with a red star. She stuck it to Walter's fur.

Walter looked at *his* star, then at Jane's and Michael's.

'It's all right, Walter,' explained Andrew. 'A red star is like a green star, only *better*!'

Mervyn's glasses

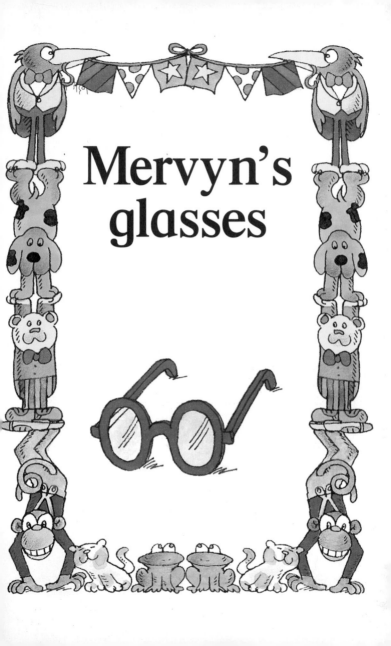

Mervyn's glasses

It was dawn. Like all night birds Mr and Mrs Owl were preparing for bed.

'I'm worried about Mervyn,' said Mrs Owl. 'I don't think he sees well.'

'You worry too much, my dear,' said Mr Owl. He snuggled up to his wife. 'Mervyn's just fine. You get a good day's sleep.'

The Owl family slept all day. At dusk they woke up, and Mr Owl flew off to work.

That night Mrs Owl watched Mervyn
carefully. She was right. Mervyn *couldn't* see
well. He didn't always empty his plate. He
held his new book too close to his eyes.

At bedtime Mrs Owl spoke to her husband
again. 'Tomorrow,' she told him, 'you must fly
over to Mr Specs. He'll soon put Mervyn right.'

When Mervyn woke up, Mrs Owl explained
the plan.

13

'But I DON'T WANT TO WEAR GLASSES,' said Mervyn. 'They'll fall down my beak. They'll make me look silly.'

'You'll look very handsome,' said Mrs Owl. 'Your father wears glasses and there's nothing wrong with *his* looks!'

'But Dad's OLD,' said Mervyn. Then he blushed. He didn't want to offend his parents.

Mervyn enjoyed the visit to Mr Specs.
Mr Specs tested his eyes with all kinds of
charts and lenses.

'This is fun,' thought Mervyn. He liked
sorting out the shapes and colours.

The next week he went to collect his
glasses. Mr Specs held up a big mirror, and
Mervyn saw himself clearly for the first time.

'What a fine bird I am!' he thought. 'BUT
I DON'T LIKE MY GLASSES.'

On the way home Mervyn noticed all kinds of new things.

'Look at the stars. See those glow worms,' he shouted. 'These glasses work a treat.'

But when he got home, Mervyn caught sight of himself in the mirror. 'SILLY OLD GLASSES!' he said to himself, stamping up and down his branch crossly.

At that moment the postman arrived.
'Special delivery,' he said, and handed
Mervyn a letter.

'What lovely big writing,' said Mervyn.
'It's an invitation,' he told his parents.
'To David's party. But I'm not going…
NOT IN THESE GLASSES!'

All week Mr and Mrs Owl tried to
persuade Mervyn. 'Please go to the party,'
they said. 'All your friends will be there. You
don't want to disappoint David.'

On the night of the party, Mervyn's parents tried one last time.

Mervyn shook his head.

'Well,' said Dad. 'If you don't want to play games and win prizes and eat a party tea, then that's up to you. I only wish I could go!'

Mervyn started to think about all the other owls having fun. In the end, he went to David's party. He brushed his feathers and

wrapped the present. Then he flew there –
all by himself.

David was waiting on *his* branch to greet
Mervyn.

Mervyn landed gracefully and held out
the present. When he looked up shyly, he
got a really super surprise!

David was wearing glasses, too. And he
looked *so* handsome!

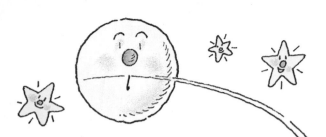

I wonder

I'm riding along in my spaceship
For all the world to see.
I've left the Earth behind–
Now what's in front of me?

The moon flies by, the planets spin,
I'm speeding through the stars.
It's Mars I want to land on.
I WONDER, what happens on Mars?

At home I've got a rabbit.
I love to play with cars.
Does Mars have pets and highways?
I WONDER, what happens on Mars?

21

My favourite food is jelly,
And peanut butter in jars.
Do Martians have their special treats?
I WONDER, what happens on Mars?

I'm riding along in my spaceship
And Mars is plain to see.
But Mum's just shouted 'TEA-TIME' –
I WONDER, what's for tea?

The queue

The queue

It was Monday morning. The doctor's waiting room was full. The patients were trying to be patient.

The nurse gave them each a card with a number. The number showed their place in the queue.

Number One was a tortoise. He held a tissue to his nose. 'I dink it's a cold,' he sniffed.

Number Two was a cat. She rubbed the fur near her tummy. 'I ate too much,' she groaned.

Number Three was a rabbit. One long ear was wrapped in a bandage. 'I hate earache,' she complained. 'It hurts to hop.'

Number Four was a small dog. His leg was in a splint. 'I MUST be better for Sports Day,' he yapped.

Number Five was a mouse. She didn't look at all well.

The tortoise, the cat, the rabbit and the dog all stared at the mouse. The nurse peeked through her window.

'I think it's DON'T-WANT-TO-GO-TO-SCHOOL-ITIS,' whispered the mouse.

The patients looked shocked. The nurse smiled.

'In that case,' said the nurse, *'Number Five* can go in *first.'*

'Good idea!' said the tortoise, the cat, the rabbit and the dog. 'Someone with WHATEVER-IT-IS-ITIS must see the doctor STRAIGHTAWAY!'

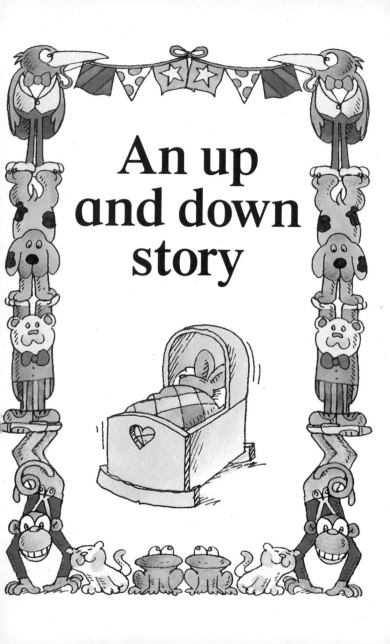

An up
and down
story

An up and down story

Mrs Kangaroo was on top of the world.
She had a brand new baby. The baby was
called Clifford.

Mrs Kangaroo rang up her friend. 'Come
and see my son,' she said.

The friend hopped over right away. She
brought a big book on child care. 'I can give
you some tips as well,' she said. 'I've got
three children of my own.'

Mrs Kangaroo listened to her friend's advice. She read the book carefully. More than anything she wanted to be a good mother.

Clifford settled down quickly. He slept at night. He gurgled through the day.

'Being a Mum is easy,' thought Mrs Kangaroo. 'It's time to get out and about.' She telephoned her friend. 'We'll hop over for coffee,' she said.

Mrs Kangaroo dressed Clifford in his best clothes and popped him in her pouch. She set off at top speed.

But before she got to the end of the road, Clifford started wailing. He'd never made that dreadful noise before. Whatever could be the matter?

Mrs Kangaroo lifted Clifford out of her pouch. She remembered everything she had read in the book.

She checked Clifford carefully, but Clifford was clean and dry. He didn't have wind.

Suddenly Mrs Kangaroo noticed Clifford's face. It wasn't kangaroo-coloured at all. Clifford's face was bright green!

Mrs Kangaroo was alarmed. Clifford must have the horrible disease the book had mentioned. It was called *Travel Sickness* and it affected very young kangaroos.

Sadly Mrs Kangaroo tiptoed the rest of the way to her friend's. She went as smoothly as she could, but it's difficult for a kangaroo not to hop at all.

By the time Mrs Kangaroo arrived, Clifford was in bad shape. His mother needed that cup of coffee.

'It's nothing to worry about,' said the friend.
'Get some BOUNCEWELL medicine.'

Mrs Kangaroo went straight to the chemist's
and bought some. 'Put a teaspoonful in
Clifford's next bottle,' advised the chemist.

After Clifford's feed Mrs Kangaroo set
off hopefully for the shops. But the medicine
didn't work. Clifford wailed all afternoon.

When she got home, Mrs Kangaroo rang her friend. 'That medicine you told me about is *no good*,' she complained. 'Clifford's all green again and I don't know *what* to do.'

'Clifford will soon grow out of it,' said the friend. 'Lots of baby kangaroos get travel sickness.'

But Mrs Kangaroo couldn't wait for Clifford to grow out of it. She didn't want to be stuck at home all day. Being a Mum wasn't so easy after all. Someone should have warned her.

Crossly, Mrs Kangaroo began to turn out her cupboards. Suddenly she found her old roller skates.

Mrs Kangaroo got very excited. Could this be the answer to Clifford's problems?

The next day Mrs Kangaroo took Clifford for a trial run. She crossed her fingers for luck because she didn't know *what* was going to happen.

Wheeeee… Mrs Kangaroo set off down the street. She soon got the hang of her skates again. Clifford had never had such a smooth ride.

In no time at all Mrs Kangaroo was halfway across town. The baby's face was still a beautiful kangaroo colour and Mum wasn't stuck at home.

But Mrs Kangaroo was careful not to skate past the police station. She would *hate* to get arrested for speeding!

Off to the park

We're off to the park,
For a bit of a lark,
I think we'll start on the slide.
We'll whizz very fast,
I WON'T be the last,
Or take the skin off my hide.

We'll swing on the swings,
And big rubber rings,
We'll point our toes to the sun.
The roundabout calls,
I hope no one falls,
The HIPPOS are on the run.

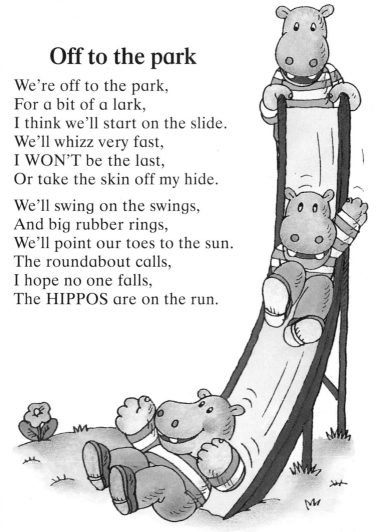

The climbing frame shudders,
The see-saw judders,
The park keeper comes to see.
'You hippos are rough –
Enough is enough –
You better go home for tea!'

Gobble gobble, yum yum

Gobble gobble, yum yum

'Where are we going for my birthday?' asked Godfrey.

'Just you wait and see,' said Mrs Goat.

Basil and Arthur arrived. 'Where are we going, Mrs Goat?' they asked.

Mrs Goat wouldn't tell.

Mrs Goat, Godfrey, Basil and Arthur set off. They passed the park.

'I know,' said Godfrey. 'We're going to the swings.'

Mrs Goat shook her head. Next they came to the sports centre.

'I know,' said Basil. 'We're going swimming.'

Mrs Goat shook her head. In the distance was a building with posters.

'I know,' said Arthur. 'We're going to the cinema.'

Mrs Goat shook her head.

At last the goats arrived.

'Here we are,' said Mrs Goat.

Godfrey, Basil and Arthur read the sign.

'GYPSY JOE'S SCRAPYARD,' it said. Whatever kind of treat was this?

'Come inside,' said Gypsy Joe. 'I'm spring cleaning.'

Joe's scrap was stacked in two neat piles. One was labelled GOOD RUBBISH and the other GOOD RIDDANCE.

Joe pointed to the GOOD RIDDANCE pile. 'Help yourselves,' he said to the goats.

The goats rushed at the rubbish. Godfrey gobbled a worn tyre. Basil chewed a cardboard box. Arthur crunched an empty can.

It took a long time to clear the GOOD RIDDANCE pile. But Godfrey, Basil and Arthur had to agree, it made a wonderful party treat.